BABY TATTOO BOOKS®
Los Angeles

SO GOOD
—FOR—
LITTLE BUNNIES

Brandi Milne

I love you, mom.

–bm

ISBN: 978-0-9793307-4-2

First Edition

10 9 8 7 6 5 4 3 2 1

Published by Baby Tattoo Books®
Los Angeles
www.babytattoo.com

Design by Laurie Young

Manufactured in China

SO GOOD
—FOR—
LITTLE BUNNIES

Hup

Hup

Summer is so good for little bunnies...
No school, no chores, no bedtime –

no problem.

Be Be and Ginger Finley knew it,
as all they had was time on their hands.

Help yourself,
Cowboy

(Loafing around *rules.*)

They heard music from a distance
come floating about on a summer breeze.
Soft and Sweet.
And the smell of fresh baked cuppy cups
and strawberry ice cream
brought Be Be to her bunny feet.

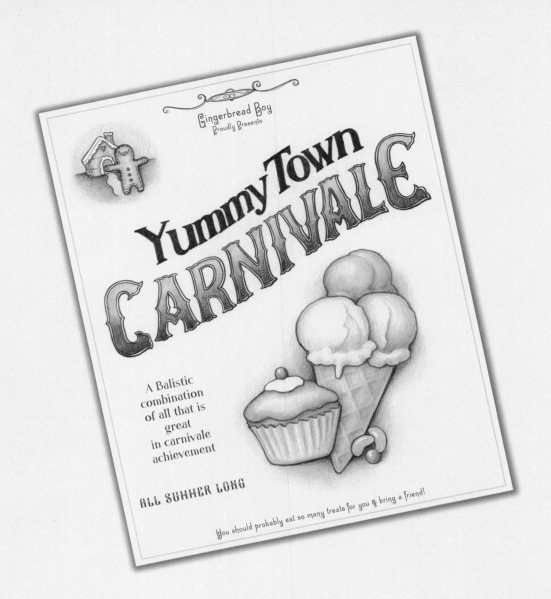

She knew it was "Yummy Town Carnivale", that came 'round every year, filling the air with its deliciousness.

And with her best doll, Be Be so wished she could go.

There's a lunatic in the grass!

Maybe just this once.

She wondered aloud, "Do you think we could go?
Is it dangerous at all?"

And just at that moment, she heard the grass move.
(A big oaf can never hide well.)
Hoxsie Clark – his monstrous looks would have
made anyone uneasy, but Be Be, she never did care.
Their friendship was awesome.
What more could she ask than to have him go with her?
Yummy Town would surely be great fun
for the three of them together.

Thumbs up and high fives were let loose everywhere!

Upon their leaving, the tune twirled
and spun with much delight.

"Captain Solo's Fresh Lemonade" was first on the mark,
where they enjoyed a cool drink and a laugh.

The Captain himself would've liked to go too,
but much work had to be done.

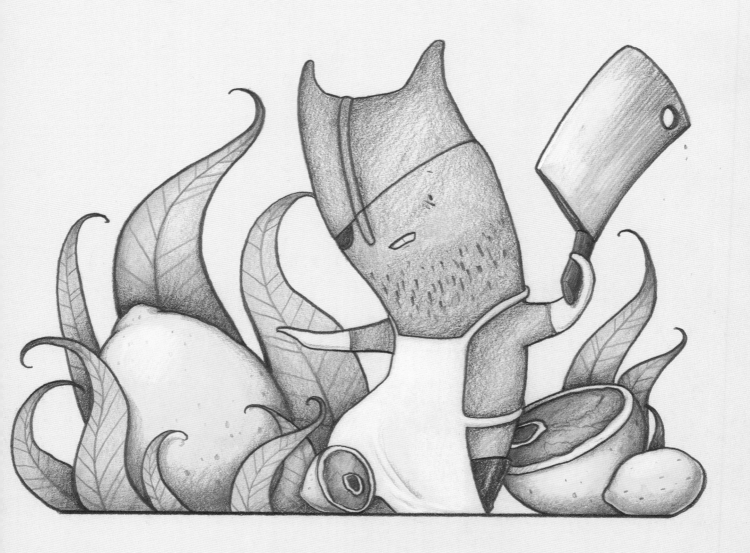

He promised them they'd never go thirsty at all,
and winked his only good eye.

From there the journey was long and peculiar —
strange things occurred...

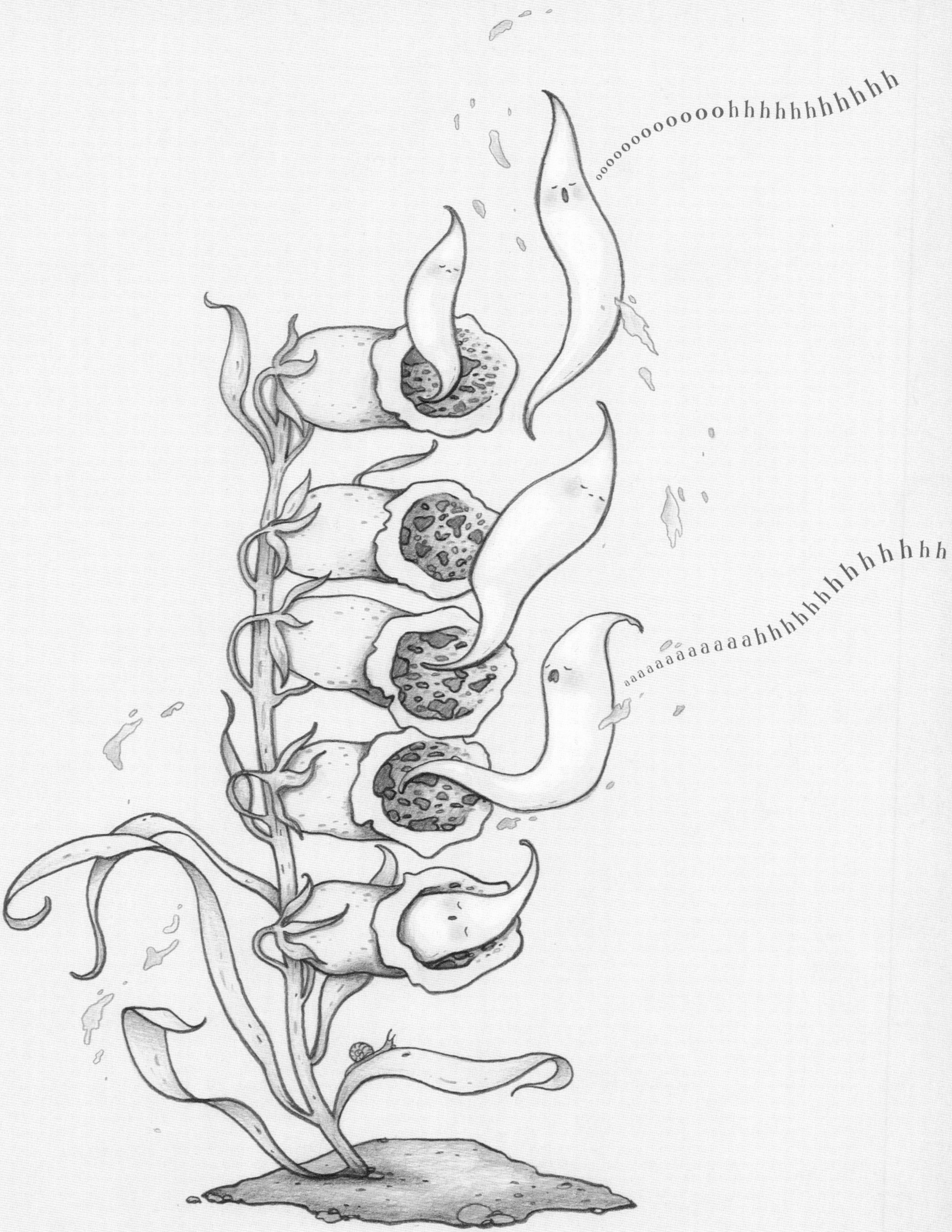
oooooooooooohhhhhhhhhhh
aaaaaaaaaaaahhhhhhhhhhhh

Like "Pork Cakes"...

Fresh Baked
Pork Cakes
The Best You Ever Ate

(wretch)

Like rock stars...

Like black birds with summer squash...

This gypsy moment...

The Fortune Queen of New Orleans

Gypsy Seeing

Amazing
Things

And Scottsborough Sly.

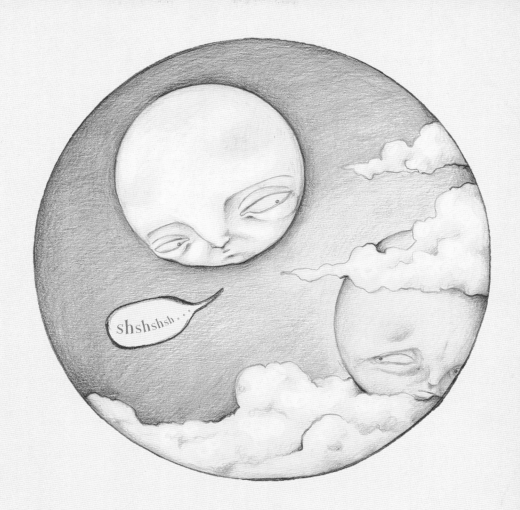

They really were on the boot heels
of some very good times.
But wind came in colder and swept through
the land — switching the daytime
into night.

There in the moonlight, they all settled in —

Be Be was worried to be far from home.
She wondered if she had been right to have gone,
and tucked herself close to her friend.

Dreams of Yummy Town sprinkled their heads,
as they slept there as cute as can be.

(yum)

Morning rose with root beer floats and Captain Solo
staring them blank in the face.

The familiar tune danced and seemed to call out,
"This way! This way!"
They hustled along with their drinks.

Soon, deep in the thick of a forest,
they found themselves huddled with fear.

A THUNDEROUS ROAR broke through the leaves
sending them trembling all about!

And out of all the sick gnarled trees,
the Surliest of Surly Giants came BLUNDERING
and STOMPING with rage!

Hideous and stenchous and gross as all that,
the Beast wrenched itself forward to pound them all out!

And just as it reached up in the air with
fists of fury driven with hate...

This scampered by.

(I know it sounds ridiculous)

It was the best thing that could have
happened at that point.

They began hooting with laughter and dancing
and making tee shirts in a hurry!

The Beast bent down and tickled each one,
and invited them over for "Ice Cream Deluxe".

They gleefully followed their new friend where she went,
laughter still stinging their cheeks.

And up the forest and out of the hill,
their destination not too much further...

The Beast said with such a big grin,

"I hope you critters like this as I do!"
then cleared the bushes for them to see...

Yummy Town Carnivale, right there before them.
Wonder. Greatness. Awe.

The four of them held their breath in their chests,
so happy – they had no words.

Be Be just stood there, her heart full of joy,
not wanting this moment
to end.

Her eyes swelled up with tears as she thought of her very best friends.
How grateful she was to be there with them...

Summer is so good for little bunnies.

Finis